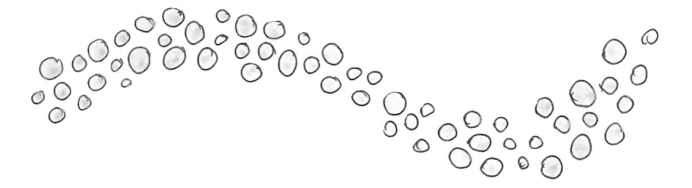

Copyright © 2018 Nicole Sigur

All rights reserved.

ISBN-13: 978-0999801130
ISBN-10: 0999801139

Every morning in aisle six, the piggy banks are arranged neatly on the shelf. Each piggy bank comes with two shiny pennies.

One energetic piggy bank always missed roll call.
His name was **Koppig.**

Unlike his friends, Koppig didn't care much for change. Instead, Koppig loved to run.

He would run down the aisle. He would run around the other toys. Sometimes, he even ran in a zigzag.

One day, Koppig heard toys yelling.

"We're better!" said a truck.

"No, we're better!" said an action figure.

The aisle seven toys decided to have a triathlon to see which toys are faster.

"A race!" Koppig exclaimed.

Koppig ran back to his place on the shelf. He quickly dug through his collection of sweatbands. He had to choose the perfect one for the race tomorrow.

"What are you so happy about?" asked a neighboring piggy bank.

"I'm going to be in a race," said Koppig.

"You can't be in a race, silly. Piggy banks just hold change. Here, I'll give you my two cents to get you started."

The piggy bank placed two cents in Koppig's slot.

"Thank you for your two cents," Koppig said with a smile, "but I am still going to enter the race."

The next morning, the trucks and action figures prepared for the race. Koppig had been up all night training. He made his way over to aisle seven. All of the toys stopped and stared.

"Are you lost, little piggy bank?" asked an action figure.

"I am here for the race," Koppig said, adjusting his sweatband.

"You can't be in a race, silly. Piggy banks just hold change. Here, I'll give you my two cents to get you started."

The action figure placed two pennies from his demo pack into Koppig's slot.

"Thank you for your two cents, but I would still like to enter the race," Koppig replied.

The aisle seven toys shrugged, and they all took their place at the starting line.

The announcer's voice echoed. "We're going to have the first of three races today - the short race. The first toy to cross the finish line wins."

Koppig squirmed in place. The announcer blew his horn and the toys took off.

The trucks spun their wheels and the action figures sprinted. Koppig had another idea.

He took a deep breath through his snout, took out his cork, and let out a big **whoosh!**

He flew through the air and landed in first place.

"Winner!" said the announcer.

All of aisle seven was in shock. They did not like when toys did things differently. Koppig stood proudly at the finish line. He didn't even notice that the other toys were upset.

Koppig started training for the second race. "I'll practice my jumping and leaping."

He stacked piles of candy on top of each other. Then, he jump, jump, jumped!

"What are you doing?" asked a candy dispenser.

"I'm training for the next race," Koppig said.

"You can't be in a race, silly. Piggy banks just hold change. Here, I'll give you my two cents to get you started."

The dispenser placed two chocolate coins into Koppig's slot.

"Thank you for your two cents, but I am still going to train for the race," Koppig replied.

Koppig made his way back to aisle seven.

The aisle seven toys couldn't believe that Koppig returned.

The announcer's voice echoed. "Welcome back, racers! Today, you will run in a hurdle race. First toy to cross the finish line wins."

Koppig was so happy to see the hurdles. He knew exactly what to do.

Koppig fluffed his cork and hopped his way down the racetrack.

Boing, *boing,* *boing!*

He landed in first place. The announcer's voice echoed,

"**winner!**"

The other toys were very upset.

The toys crowded around Koppig. One by one, they filled his slot with their two cents.

Koppig spent the next morning on the shelf with the other piggy banks. He was too full of change to go for his morning run. The other piggy banks grew concerned.

"Aren't you going to be late for the third race?" asked another piggy bank.

"I'm feeling *really* heavy today," slumped Koppig. "I don't think I'm going to go."

"That's a shame. You made all of that running and jumping look so fun. We planned on watching you race."

Koppig perked up a bit. "Really? Hm. I guess the least that I could do is go watch."

The announcer's voice echoed. "Today, we will do the long race. First toy to the finish line wins."

The toys took off down the aisle. The crowd cheered. Koppig sat in a cloud of dust at the starting line.

Koppig was so full of everyone's two cents that he wasn't sure if he could run.

"Maybe I don't have to accept everyone's two cents," Koppig thought to himself. "There is nothing wrong with being different."

Koppig placed his hoof over his cork and pulled as hard as he could. All of the two cents that people had given him fell to the ground.

Koppig felt so much lighter that he started running down the aisle.

ZOOM!

He ran past all of the trucks and all of the action figures, and landed in **first place**.

The crowd roared. They could not believe how quickly Koppig had made it down the aisle.

"You really do belong here," a truck said.

"I never saw a piggy bank run so fast!" said the candy dispenser.

"What's your secret?" asked an action figure.

Koppig smiled, and looked back at the pile of change in the distance.

"I just stayed true to myself. Sometimes, **two cents** aren't worth the weight."

50628157R00018

Made in the USA
Middletown, DE
26 June 2019